A Kiss

Level 1C

Written by Anne Marie Ryan
Illustrated by Florencia Denis

Ticktock

What is synthetic phonics?

Synthetic phonics teaches children to recognise the sounds of letters and to blend (synthesise) them together to make whole words.

Understanding sound/letter relationships gives children the confidence and ability to read unfamiliar words, without having to rely on memory or guesswork; this helps them progress towards independent reading.

Did you know? Spoken English uses more than 40 speech sounds. Each sound is called a *phoneme*. Some phonemes relate to a single letter (d-o-g) and others to combinations of letters (sh-ar-p). When a phoneme is written down it is called a *grapheme*. Teaching these sounds, matching them to their written form and sounding out words for reading is the basis of synthetic phonics.

Consultant

I love reading phonics has been created in consultation with language expert Abigail Steel. She has a background in teaching and teacher training and is a respected expert in the field of Synthetic Phonics. Abigail Steel is a regular contributor to educational publications. Her international education consultancy supports parents and teachers in the promotion of literacy skills.

Reading tips

This book focuses on the sounds:
qu, x, ff, ll, ss, zz and ck.

Tricky words in this book

Any words in bold may have unusual spellings or are
new and have not yet been introduced.

> ### Tricky words in this book:
>
> **the   to   who   he**
> **you   me   says   I**

Extra ways to have fun with this book

After the reader has finished the story, ask them
questions about what they have just read:

Who does Nick try to kiss?
Why does Nick get into a huff?

Make flashcards of the focus sounds (qu, x, ff, ll, ss,
zz and ck). Ask the reader to say the words, sounding
them out. This will help reinforce letter/sound matches.

My big brother
listens to me read.
He says I'm a very good
reader. I like to read
in his bedroom.

A pronunciation guide

This grid highlights the sounds used in the story and offers a guide on how to say them.

s as in sat	**a** as in ant	**t** as in tin	**p** as in pig
i as ink	**n** as in net	**c** as in cat	**e** as in egg
h as in hen	**r** as in rat	**m** as in mug	**d** as in dog
g as in get	**o** as in ox	**u** as in up	**l** as in log
f as in fan	**b** as in bag	**j** as in jug	**v** as in van
w as in wet	**z** as in zip	**y** as in yet	**k** as in kit
qu as in quiz	**x** as in box	**ff** as in off	**ll** as in fill
ss as in hiss	**zz** as in buzz	**ck** as in duck	

Be careful not to add an 'uh' sound to 's', 't', 'p', 'c', 'h', 'r', 'm', 'd', 'g', 'l', 'f' and 'b'. For example, say 'fff' not 'fuh' and 'sss' not 'suh'.

Nick **the** duck sits on a dock.

Bugs buzz and kiss.

Nick is off **to** get a kiss.

Who will **he** pick?

'Will **you** kiss **me**?' **says** Nick.

'Buzz off,' says an ox on the hill.

'Kiss me, quick!' says Nick.

'**I** will pass,' says a hen on a box.

'Can I just get a kiss?' says Nick.

'Back off,' says a cat on a rock.

'Kiss?' says Nick.

'Yuck!' says a fox as he zips off.

Nick is in a huff!

But Nick is in luck!

Viv is at the well.

Peck!
Nick has a kiss on his bill.

'Quack!' says Nick.

OVER 48 TITLES IN SIX LEVELS
Abigail Steel recommends...

Other titles to enjoy from Level 1

Bad Rat
978-1-84898-600-8

The Best Gift
978-1-84898-603-9

Gran and Bret's Trip
978-1-78325-100-1

Some titles from Level 2

Wish Fish
978-1-84898-604-6

Chuck and Duck
978-1-84898-605-3

Pink Bunny
978-1-78325-103-2

Let's go to the Swings
978-1-78325-102-5

Some titles from Level 3

Bart's Go-Cart
978-1-78325-105-6

Queen Ella's Feet
978-1-84898-609-1

Puff Flies
978-1-84898-610-7

The Pop Duet
978-1-78325-108-7

An Hachette UK Company
www.hachette.co.uk
Copyright © Octopus Publishing Group Ltd 2012
First published in Great Britain in 2012 by TickTock, an imprint of Octopus Publishing Group Ltd,
Endeavour House, 189 Shaftesbury Avenue, London WC2H 8JY.
www.octopusbooks.co.uk
www.ticktockbooks.co.uk
ISBN 978 1 84898 602 2
Printed and bound in China
10 9 8 7 6 5 4 3